Miss March

Miss March lived in a castle.

She planted trees in her garden.

She put sharks in the moat.

It was hard to get up the mast,
but that didn't stop Miss March!
She looked down into the yard.

Nan parked her car in the yard.

"Hello!" Miss March yelled down
to Nan.

Nan was alarmed. She had to cross
the moat on a raft.

"Sharks have sharp teeth," she said.

Miss March and Nan played cards
by the hearth. Then they jumped
up and started to dance.

Nan loved Miss March with all her
heart, but she was glad to get back.
"No sharks in my yard!" she said.

Questions for discussion:

- What was unusual about Miss March?

- What did Miss March and Nan do together?

- Why do you think Nan was glad to get back home?

Game with /ar/ words

Play as 'Concentration' or use for reading practice. Enlarge and photocopy the page twice on two different colors of card.
Cut the cards up to play.
Ensure the players sound out the words.

car	bark	start
park	heart	garden
shark	dark	far
farm	star	hearth

Before reading this book, the reader needs to know:

- sounds can be spelled by more than one letter.
- the spellings <ar> and <ear> can represent the sound /ar/.

This book introduces:

- the spellings <ar> and <ear> for the sound /ar/.
- text at 2-syllable level.

Words the reader may need help with:

lived, castle, trees, her, put, moat, was, looked, down, into, hello, teeth, said, played, by, they, dance, loved, all

Vocabulary:

moat — a deep ditch round a castle, usually filled with water
mast — a tall pole that holds up a flag
alarmed - frightened
hearth — the floor around a fireplace

Talk about the story:

Miss March invites Nan to visit her in her castle. Nan finds out that nothing is boring in Miss March's castle...

Reading Practice

Practice blending these sounds into words:

ar	ear
car	heart
dark	hearth
far	
hard	
garden	
park	
start	